The Symphony Within: A Journey Through Chaos and Resilience

By Dr. Shabina Sheth

The Symphony Within: A Journey Through Chaos and Resilience

Author: Dr. Shabina Sheth

Publisher: Self-published by Dr. Shabinabegam Abdul Majid Sheth (Dr. Shabina Sheth)

ISBN: [978-93-342-2647-8]

Printed in various locations worldwide based on the platform's print-on-demand services.

Cover Design by **Dr. Shabinabegam Abdul Majid Sheth**

For permissions or inquiries, contact: dr.shabinasheth@gmail.com

Dedication

To my son, Muhammed Khizar Ibrahim, who fills my world with music; and to my patients, whose courage to heal inspires me every day.

Contents

Chapter 1: The Hummingbird

Elias played the piano like a man in a dream—a vivid, unstoppable dream that blurred the line between brilliance and chaos. It wasn't just music spilling out of him; it was a torrent of emotions, each note carrying a piece of his soul. Jazz bled into classical, then twisted into blues and folk, creating a dizzying storm of sound. His hands, a blur on the keys, seemed to chase an idea that was always just out of reach. His body swayed with the rhythm, jerking unpredictably as if it, too, was caught in the storm.

He looked wild—sweat streaming down his face, his hair disheveled, and his eyes wide and unseeing. Yet he was smiling, a manic, electric grin that hinted at the fire raging inside him.

Elias wasn't typically like this. He was quiet, someone who moved through the world like a shadow. But when these surges hit, it was as if the universe itself flowed through him. He didn't feel tired, not even after three sleepless nights. The need for rest seemed like a foreign concept. Instead, his energy felt infinite, spilling into every corner of his life.

His apartment bore the marks of this unrelenting force. Canvases lay abandoned on the floor, streaked with frenzied brushstrokes that defied interpretation. Sheets of music covered in half-scribbled notes were strewn everywhere, competing for space with an army of coffee cups—some empty, some forgotten in mid-sip. The place no longer felt like a home but a battlefield of ideas, every surface a casualty of his relentless need to create.

But there was fear lurking beneath the surface of this whirlwind. Briefly, his father's voice echoed in his mind: *"Why can't you be normal?"* The words stung, as they always did, but he shoved them aside, determined not to let them pull him under.

He barely registered the pounding on his door or the muffled voice of Mrs. Rodriguez, his downstairs neighbor, yelling about the noise. The music rose louder, blocking out the world, until suddenly, it stopped.

Elias froze. His hands hovered over the piano, trembling. The silence that followed felt heavier than the music, like a wave crashing down on him. His vision dimmed as the vibrant colors in his mind faded to gray.

Exhaustion hit him like a physical blow, draining every ounce of energy from his body. He slumped forward, his head landing heavily on the piano keys with a dull, discordant thud. His last conscious memory was the faint sound of Mrs. Rodriguez's voice, closer now, and the sight of her anxious face peeking through his doorway.

Dr. Julian Vance arrived at the apartment not long after, stepping into the wreckage Elias had left behind. Broken brushes, splattered paint, coffee-stained papers—it was a familiar scene. He'd seen this kind of destruction many times before, though it never failed to strike a chord in him.

He knelt and picked up a sheet of music from the floor, its scrawled notes barely legible. To him, it was more than a mess. It was a reflection of the turmoil inside Elias's mind—a fragile genius caught in the grip of something both beautiful and destructive.

Julian adjusted his glasses, a small gesture that gave him a moment to gather his thoughts. Years of working as a psychiatrist had honed his ability to remain calm and patient, even in the face of tragedy. But Elias's situation tugged at something deeper.

He saw more than a young man consumed by mania. He saw a flicker of defiance in Elias, a resilience fighting to survive beneath the chaos. He thought of the journey ahead—long, winding, and full of uncertainty. It wouldn't be easy. Medication, therapy, and time would all play their parts. But as Julian turned to leave the apartment, he couldn't shake the image of Elias slumped over the piano.

There was a story here, Julian thought—a story of struggle and hope, of a mind battling its own brilliance. And this was only the beginning.

The apartment was silent now, but Mrs. Rodriguez still couldn't sleep. She sat in her living room, her hands clasped tightly as she stared at the ceiling. The noise had been unbearable earlier, pounding through her walls until she couldn't take it anymore.

Elias wasn't a bad kid, she thought. In fact, he was one of the few tenants she actually liked. He was always polite, always asked about her grandchildren. But when he got into one of his moods, it was as if he became a different person.

She had marched upstairs, ready to give him a piece of her mind. But the moment she opened the door, all her anger melted away. The sight of him slumped over the piano, his body still and his face pale, sent a chill through her.

"Mijo..." she had whispered, stepping cautiously into the room. She didn't understand why he pushed himself like this, why he let himself spiral so far out of control. But as she stood there, taking in the chaos around her, one thing was clear—Elias needed help.

Chapter 2: Fragments of a Symphony

Elias awoke to a strange, sterile quiet, the rhythmic beeping of a heart monitor his only companion. The world around him felt alien—too white, too still, a stark contrast to the vibrant symphony of his mind just hours before. He blinked, disoriented, his body leaden, his thoughts moving sluggishly, like trying to swim through tar.

The colors and energy that had consumed him were gone now, replaced by an ache so hollow it felt as if it might swallow him whole.

"Elias?"

The voice was soft, kind, drawing his attention to the woman seated beside his bed. She had gentle eyes and a warm smile, her presence a stark contrast to the sterile hospital room. "I'm Dr. Ramirez, your psychiatrist."

He opened his mouth to reply, but all that emerged was a dry rasp. She held out a cup of water, steadying it as he sipped.

"You had a manic episode," she explained gently. "It's important we talk about what happened."

Elias looked away, shame curling in his chest. He didn't want to talk about it, didn't want to relive the wild energy, the relentless drive that had consumed him—or the exhaustion and collapse that followed. The memory of Mrs. Rodriguez's worried face flashed in his mind, and he turned further away, his gaze fixed on the wall.

"I'm just tired," he mumbled, though the weight pressing on him was much more than fatigue. He hated this—being vulnerable, being seen as broken. He wanted to be Elias the musician, not Elias the patient.

"It's okay to feel that way," Dr. Ramirez said softly, as if reading his thoughts. "You're here now, and we're going to help you."

Her words were meant to comfort, but they only deepened the ache in his chest. Help. Manage. Stability. Each sounded like a prison sentence. He closed his eyes, the word "illness" echoing in his mind. He wasn't an illness. He was an artist, a creator, someone who lived in color and sound—not the gray monotony Dr. Ramirez seemed to offer.

The days blurred together, a haze of medications, blood tests, and therapy sessions. Dr. Ramirez was kind and straightforward, walking him through the diagnosis: bipolar disorder. She described the pendulum swing between manic highs and crushing lows, the unpredictability, the need for treatment and support.

Elias listened, nodding in the right places, but her words washed over him like background noise. His mind kept circling back to the same thought: *What would this mean for his music?*

Dr. Vance, the psychiatrist who had first entered his chaotic apartment, visited often. He was different from Dr. Ramirez—quieter, more observant. Instead of talking *to* Elias, he listened, his questions subtle but piercing.

One afternoon, Dr. Vance handed him a slim, weathered book of poetry. “I thought you might like this,” he said, his voice calm and measured. “Sylvia Plath struggled with bipolar disorder, too. Her work is... honest. Raw.”

Elias took the book, his fingers brushing the worn cover. He opened it to a random page and read aloud:

"The moon is my mother. She is not sweet like Mary. Her blue garments unloose small bats and owls."

The words were sharp, vivid, cutting through the fog in his mind. For the first time in days, Elias felt something stir within him. The rhythm, the imagery—they spoke to a part of him that hadn’t disappeared entirely, even in the hospital.

He devoured the poems, each one pulling him closer to a strange sense of understanding. Plath’s darkness mirrored his own, but her words carried defiant beauty, as if she’d captured chaos and turned it into art.

By the end of the week, Elias was well enough to sit in the hospital’s recreation room, a drab space with mismatched furniture and an out-of-tune piano. He approached it hesitantly, his fingers brushing the yellow keys.

The first note was tentative, uncertain. But as he played, the music began to flow, haltingly at first, then with more confidence. He wasn’t chasing the wild, uncontrollable melodies of his manic state. Instead, the music was quieter, more reflective—a tapestry of notes that echoed both his pain and his hope.

When he looked up, he noticed Chloe, a fellow patient, watching him from across the room. Her green eyes sparkled with quiet curiosity. "You play beautifully," she said, her voice low but steady.

Elias smiled faintly. "Thanks," he said, his fingers hovering over the keys. "Do you play?"

She gestured to the violin case resting on a chair beside her. "It's been a while, but... yeah."

Their conversation was halting, peppered with long silences. But as they spoke, Elias felt an unexpected connection to Chloe, her presence a calm counterpoint to his restless thoughts.

Before he returned to his room, she suggested they play together someday. He nodded, feeling the faintest flicker of something he hadn't dared hope for in a long time: the possibility of friendship.

Chapter 3: The Red Violin

The crisp autumn air greeted Elias as he stepped out of the hospital, crisp and full of earthy smells that hinted at falling leaves and damp soil. He stopped on the sidewalk, unsure of where to go. Freedom wasn't what he'd imagined—not light or liberating, but something fragile and unwieldy. It felt as though the world had shifted while he was away, leaving him out of sync.

The prescription slip and a list of support groups sat in his pocket, their edges crisp and sharp against his fingers whenever he touched them. They were practical tools for recovery, but they felt more like lifelines tethering him to a world he wasn't sure he belonged to anymore.

The city around him moved as it always did—impatient drivers honking, people hurrying along with their lives. Elias walked aimlessly, his body moving while his mind drifted. The idea of returning to his apartment, still wrecked from his manic episode, felt overwhelming. He couldn't yet face the mess he had made, both within those walls and inside himself.

After a while, he found himself in a small park. It was tucked between towering buildings, a quiet refuge from the chaos of the city. The benches were scattered with fallen leaves, their vibrant oranges and reds softened by the low afternoon sun. For the first time that day, Elias felt something other than unease—a faint sense of calm.

Then he heard it—a melody, haunting and bittersweet. It floated through the air, a delicate sound that tugged at him, drawing him closer. He followed the music until he saw her: a young woman standing beneath a sprawling oak tree, her violin tucked beneath her chin.

She moved with the music, swaying gently as her bow danced across the strings. Her fiery red hair glinted in the sunlight, and her eyes were closed as if she, too, was being carried away by the melody.

Elias stopped, captivated. The music wasn't just beautiful; it was alive, raw and filled with longing. It stirred something deep within him, a flicker of the passion he thought he'd lost. For a moment, he simply stood there, listening, until the final note faded into the cool autumn breeze.

He took a hesitant step forward. "Chloe?"

Her eyes opened wide with surprise. "Elias! What are you doing here?"

"I... I could ask you the same thing," he replied, his voice quieter than he intended.

Chloe rested the violin at her side, brushing a stray strand of hair from her face. "I come here to play sometimes. It clears my head."

Elias nodded, understanding immediately. Music had always been his refuge too, a way to make sense of the chaos within.

They found a bench nearby and sat down. Chloe placed her violin carefully on the grass, its red lacquer gleaming in the fading light.

"Do you always play like that?" Elias asked after a moment.

She shrugged, a faint smile tugging at her lips. "Only when I feel like I have something to say. I guess I don't always have the words, but the music... it speaks for me."

Elias hesitated, his fingers playing with the frayed edge of his coat sleeve. "I know what you mean. Sometimes, it feels like the only thing that makes sense."

They sat in silence for a while, watching the leaves flutter down from the trees. Chloe broke the quiet, her voice soft. "Do you think... it'll ever get easier?"

Elias glanced at her, surprised by the vulnerability in her tone. "I don't know," he admitted. "But maybe it's not about easy. Maybe it's about finding a way to keep going."

Chloe looked at him, her green eyes searching his face. "I like that," she said finally. "Finding a way."

She picked up her violin, running her fingers along its polished surface. "You and I should play together sometime," she said, a mischievous grin lighting up her face. "You on the piano, me on the violin. We could call ourselves... I don't know, 'The Melancholy Melodies.'"

Elias laughed—a real, unguarded laugh that startled even him. "I like it," he said. "It has a nice ring to it."

As the sun dipped lower, painting the park in golden hues, they parted ways. Chloe tucked her violin under her arm and gave him a quick wave before disappearing down the path.

Elias stood there for a moment, watching her go. The melody of her violin lingered in his mind, blending with the rustling leaves and the soft hum of the city beyond the trees. For the first time in weeks, he felt a flicker of hope.

When he finally returned to his apartment, the sight of its chaos didn't paralyze him the way it had earlier. The canvases on the floor, the crumpled sheet music, the empty coffee cups—it was still a mess, but now it felt like a mess he could face.

Sitting at his piano, Elias touched the keys, his fingers hesitant. The first note was soft, almost tentative, but it was followed by another, and then another. Slowly, a melody emerged—imperfect but real, weaving its way through the silence of the room.

He thought of Chloe and her violin, of the way her music had stirred something within him. Maybe she was right. Maybe finding a way forward didn't have to be perfect. Maybe it just had to begin.

Chapter 4: Shadows of the Past

Elias stood in front of his apartment door, his hand hovering over the handle. A lump formed in his throat as he imagined the scene waiting on the other side. He had avoided this place since his discharge, wandering parks and libraries to escape the wreckage he'd left behind. But now, there was nowhere else to go.

Taking a deep breath, he turned the knob and stepped inside. The air was thick and stale, carrying the faint bitterness of old coffee. His eyes swept over the chaos: canvases leaned haphazardly against the walls, splattered with wild streaks of paint. Torn sheets of music lay crumpled on the floor like discarded thoughts. The piano sat in the center of it all, silent and accusatory, its keys dotted with coffee stains and a layer of dust.

It wasn't just a mess—it was a snapshot of his collapse, frozen in time. Each detail felt like a mirror reflecting his shame, his fear, his inability to control the storm within him.

Elias moved mechanically, picking up a canvas and leaning it against the wall. He started sorting the scattered sheet music, but his hands trembled, and he had to stop. His chest tightened as his gaze landed on a photo frame lying face down on the floor.

He picked it up, turning it over in his hands. The photo inside showed him as a teenager, standing stiffly beside his father. The man's stern expression was as familiar as it was haunting. Even in this freezing moment, his father's disapproval seemed to radiate from the image.

A flood of memories crashed over Elias.

He was ten years old again, sitting at the dining table with his homework spread out before him. His father loomed nearby, his arms crossed, his voice sharp. "What kind of grade is this, Elias? You can't afford to slack off like this if you want to get anywhere in life."

Elias had nodded silently, his small hands gripping his pencil tightly. He wanted to explain, to say that he'd been too distracted by the melody stuck in his head, the one he'd been trying to play on the old keyboard in his room. But he knew better than to argue.

Another memory surfaced—a more painful one. He was a teenager, standing in the living room, his fists clenched as he faced his father.

"I don't want to study economics," Elias had said, his voice trembling but defiant. "I want to make music. That's what I love."

His father's face darkened; his voice cold. "Music isn't a career, Elias. It's a hobby. If you waste your life chasing dreams, you'll end up just like your mother—unstable, unreliable, a failure."

The words hit like a slap. His mother. Elias had always known not to bring her up in arguments, but hearing his father use her as a weapon break something inside him. He stormed out of the house that day, slamming the door behind him, the sound echoing in his mind for years.

Elias stared at the photo now, his grip tightening. His father's words still haunted him, even after all this time. They had burrowed deep into his mind, feeding his doubts, fueling his fear that he would never be enough.

A wave of anger surged through him—anger at his father for never understanding, anger at himself for still craving approval that would never come. Without thinking, he hurled the frame across the room. It shattered against the wall, the glass breaking into jagged pieces that sparkled in the dim light.

The sound was sharp, cathartic. For a moment, Elias stood frozen, his breath coming in ragged gasps. Then, slowly, he sank to the floor, his head resting against the wall.

He didn't know how long he sat there, staring at the broken frame and the photo now lying amid shards of glass. His anger ebbed, leaving behind a hollow ache. But in that emptiness, there was something else—a faint flicker of resolve.

Elias knew he couldn't keep living in the shadow of his father's disapproval. The weight of it had crushed him for too long. If he was going to move forward, he had to let go of the need to prove himself to a man who would never see him for who he truly was.

He stood up, brushing off his hands, and carefully picked up the shattered pieces of glass. Each shard felt sharp against his fingers, a reminder of how easily things could break.

When the floor was clear, Elias turned to his piano. He ran his fingers over the keys, the cool ivory smooth under his touch. The notes he played were slow, deliberate—a melody not of chaos but of rebuilding.

In that moment, the room still felt heavy, the memories still painful. But there was a small, growing hope in Elias's heart. He didn't have all the answers yet, but he was beginning to understand that he didn't need to.

Letting go wouldn't happen overnight, but for the first time, it felt like it was possible.

Chapter 5: Unearthing the Roots

Elias sat stiffly in the overstuffed armchair; his hands clasped so tightly his knuckles had gone white. Dr. Vance's office had a kind of curated coziness to it—soft lighting, shelves crammed with books, and a painting of some calm, sprawling landscape above the desk. But all of that calm couldn't undo the knot of anxiety twisting in Elias's stomach.

He hated this part. The *talking* part.

"So," Dr. Vance began, his voice soft and even, "you mentioned last time that your father's reaction to your diagnosis brought up... a lot for you."

Elias let out a hollow laugh, the kind that didn't reach his eyes. "Yeah, you could say that."

Dr. Vance nodded, waiting. That's what he was good at—waiting. No rush, no judgment, just silence that stretched out long enough to make you feel like you might as well fill it.

Elias sighed, leaning back against the chair. "He said I was just like my mom. Unstable. A failure." The words felt acidic, like they burned his throat on the way out.

Dr. Vance didn't flinch, though something flickered in his expression. Was it sympathy? Disapproval? Elias wasn't sure, but he was already regretting saying anything.

"Tell me about your mom," Dr. Vance said gently.

Elias's chest tightened. He looked away, his gaze landing on the corner of the room where a pot of lavender sat on the windowsill. He focused on the plant, anything to avoid those words. "She had... struggles," he said vaguely. "You know, mental health stuff. They called it a nervous breakdown back then, but... I was just a kid. I didn't really get it."

Dr. Vance leaned forward slightly, resting his hands on his notepad. "What do you remember about her?"

For a moment, Elias was quiet. He didn't want to go there. But memories had a funny way of rising to the surface, whether you wanted them to or not.

He was eight years old, crouched behind the banister at the top of the stairs, peering through the gaps at the scene below. His mom was on the living room floor, sobbing so hard her whole body shook. His dad was standing over her, his face a storm cloud of frustration and helplessness.

"Get ahold of yourself, Clara!" his dad snapped, his voice sharp enough to cut through the walls. "This is ridiculous."

Elias didn't understand what was happening, but he felt it—the tension in the air, the way it pressed down on his small frame. He wanted to run down the stairs and hug his mom, to make her stop crying, but his dad's voice held him frozen in place.

Later that night, when his mom had finally fallen silent, he snuck into her room. She was curled up in bed, her face pale and puffy, her hair tangled around her face. She didn't say anything when he climbed onto the bed beside her, but she pulled him close, her arms trembling as she held him.

Back in Dr. Vance's office, Elias swallowed hard, his throat dry. "She was... fragile," he said finally. "But she was kind. I just remember wanting to protect her, even though I didn't know how."

Dr. Vance nodded; his expression thoughtful. "And your dad?"

Elias snorted. "What about him? He was... strong, I guess. But not in the effective way. More like a wall. You couldn't get through to him, you know? He didn't get it. He didn't want to get it."

Dr. Vance tilted his head slightly. "How do you think his reaction to your mom's struggles affected you?"

Elias hesitated, his fingers picking at the edge of his sleeve. "I don't know," he said, though the answer was sitting heavy on his chest. "I guess... I learned to keep things to myself. Like, don't bother anyone. Don't make waves."

He paused, then added bitterly, "And whatever you do, don't end up like Mom."

Dr. Vance's voice broke the silence, calm but firm. "That's a heavy burden to carry, Elias. Feeling like you have to hide your struggles, to be the opposite of someone you loved... That's a lot."

Elias blinked, the words hitting him like a punch to the gut. He hadn't thought of it that way before, but hearing it said out loud made something inside him shift.

Dr. Vance leaned back, giving him space. "It's okay to feel those emotions. The anger, the guilt, the sadness. They're part of the process. Acknowledging them is the first step toward understanding—and healing."

Elias rubbed his hands over his face, his chest tightening again. "It's just... I don't know. It feels like I'm always carrying this weight, and no matter what I do, it doesn't get lighter."

Dr. Vance nodded, his voice steady. "It won't happen overnight, Elias. But every time you confront these feelings, every time you allow yourself to process them, you're chipping away at that weight. And one day, it won't feel so heavy."

When Elias left the office that day, the air outside felt crisper, the autumn leaves brighter against the gray sky. He walked without a destination, his hands in his pockets and his mind replaying the session.

It wasn't that everything suddenly made sense. It wasn't that he felt lighter or healed or free. But for the first time, he felt like he wasn't running from his past. He was facing it—slowly, messily, but facing it, nonetheless.

He stopped at a park bench, sitting down and staring at the empty playground nearby. In his pocket, his fingers brushed against the folded-up piece of music he'd written in the hospital—a simple, melancholic melody.

Pulling it out, he smoothed the paper and studied the notes. It wasn't perfect, but it was his. Maybe that was enough for now.

Chapter 6: Duet in the Key of Hope

Elias sat in the corner of the café, fidgeting with the edge of a napkin until it was nothing more than a frayed pile of fibers. Around him, the room buzzed with soft conversation and the occasional hiss of the espresso machine. The place smelled like roasted coffee beans and cinnamon, comforting yet slightly overwhelming.

He glanced at the door for the third time in as many minutes. Chloe was late. Not that he was surprised, but his punctuality didn't seem to be her strong suit—but the wait was enough to let his nerves spiral. What if she didn't show? What if she'd changed her mind?

The bell above the door jingled, and Elias looked up, his stomach flipping. There she was her fiery red hair slightly mussed as though she'd sprinted the last block. She spotted him and waved with the kind of enthusiasm that made it impossible not to smile.

"Sorry, sorry!" Chloe said, plopping down across from him with a grin. "I swear, the universe is conspiring against me today. Traffic, this old guy in line who wanted to discuss the moral implications of oat milk... you name it."

Elias chuckled, his tension easing. "Oat milk? That's... niche."

"Right?" she said, rolling her eyes dramatically. "Anyway, I'm here now. Ready to make some melancholic magic?"

The violin case she set on the table gleamed, its red lacquer catching the light. Elias nodded toward it. “Do you always carry that around?”

“Only when I want to impress people,” she said with a wink. “Come on, let’s find a corner to jam.”

They moved to a quieter section of the café, where Elias set up his battered portable keyboard. He ran his fingers over the keys, feeling their smooth, slightly worn surface. Chloe tuned her violin, the high, clear notes cutting through the low hum of conversation.

“What should we start with?” she asked, adjusting the chinrest.

“Something simple,” Elias said. “Blues?”

Chloe’s face lit up. “Blues with a twist. Let’s add a little whimsy. We *are* the Melancholy Melodies, after all.”

Elias laughed, the sound light and unexpected. “All right. You lead, I’ll follow.”

She began with a soft, mournful note, letting it linger before sliding into a melody that was both somber and playful. Elias joined in, his chords wrapping around her violin like a conversation. The music grew, shifting and evolving as they played off each other’s cues.

It wasn’t perfect—there were hesitations, a few discordant moments—but that only made it more real. The café seemed to fade around them, the world narrowing to the music and the unspoken connection they were building.

"Do you ever feel like your brain's stuck on a broken record?" Chloe asked between songs, resting her violin on her lap.

Elias paused, considering. "You mean like the same thoughts playing over and over?"

"Yeah. Like, no matter what you do, you keep looping back to the same thing."

He nodded slowly. "I get that. It's like... you're trying to move forward, but there's this anchor pulling you back."

Chloe tilted her head, her green eyes thoughtful. "Exactly. And people say stuff like, 'Just let it go.' But they don't get that sometimes you don't *want* to let it go. Sometimes you need to hold onto it until you can figure it out."

Elias smiled faintly. "I guess that's where the music comes in."

She grinned. "Exactly. The ultimate therapy session. Cheaper than Dr. Vance, too."

As they played their final piece, Chloe leaned into the music, her bow moving faster, her notes climbing higher. Elias matched her pace, his fingers flying over the keys. The melody soared, a chaotic, beautiful swirl of emotion that felt like a release.

When the last note faded, they both sat back, breathing hard. Chloe was the first to break the silence.

"Okay," she said, grinning, "that was officially epic."

Elias laughed, the sound full and genuine. "Not bad for a first gig."

She raised an eyebrow. "First of many?"

"Yeah," he said, surprising himself with the certainty in his voice. "First of many."

Walking home that evening, Elias felt lighter than he had in months. The memory of their music lingered, weaving its way through his thoughts. It wasn't just the notes or the rhythms—it was the connection; the way Chloe had turned something as simple as a jam session into a lifeline.

As he unlocked his apartment door, he glanced at his piano. For the first time in a long time, it didn't feel like a reminder of what he'd lost. Instead, it felt like an invitation to create something new.

Chapter 7: Navigating the Gray

Elias stared at the little orange pill in his hand, the light catching its glossy surface. It was ridiculous, really—how something so small could carry so much weight. With a resigned sigh, he swallowed it, chasing it with water.

The dulling effect was gradual but unmistakable. The chaotic energy that had once powered him—both his music and his downfall—was gone. In its place was a strange stillness, not entirely unpleasant, but unnervingly hollow. It felt like standing in the middle of a quiet field, unsure of which direction to go.

Later that morning, Elias sat at the piano, his fingers resting on the keys. He pressed a single note, letting it linger in the air. It was pure, but lifeless, like a photograph of a memory instead of the memory itself.

He tried a chord, then another. The notes were correct—he could hear that—but they didn't move him. The frustration was immediate, clawing at him like an itch he couldn't scratch.

The knock on his door startled him.

"Uncle Elias!" Lily's voice rang out, bright and impatient.

He opened the door to find her bouncing on the balls of her feet, her pigtails swaying with motion. Behind her stood Rachel, her expression half-apologetic, half-amused.

"She's been on a mission all morning," Rachel said. "Apparently, you're the only person in the world who can teach her 'real' piano."

"I never said, 'only person in the world,'" Lily corrected, grinning up at him. "But, yeah, you're the best. Can we play?"

Elias stepped aside, waving them in. "How could I say no to my number one fan?"

Lily's enthusiasm was as boundless as her energy. She climbed onto the piano bench like it was a jungle gym, her legs swinging as she watched Elias with wide eyes.

"Show me something cool!" she demanded, her hands poised dramatically over the keys.

"Cool, huh?" Elias smirked. "How about this?" He played a simple blues riff, adding a few flourishes for flair.

Lily gasped, her face lighting up. "That's awesome! Okay, my turn."

Her attempt was... enthusiastic. The notes came out in a chaotic tumble, like raindrops hitting a tin roof. But the joy on her face was infectious, pulling a laugh from Elias despite himself.

"Not bad," he said, nudging her gently. "But maybe try this finger position."

As she adjusted, Lily glanced up at him. "Why don't you play like you used to?"

The question caught him off guard, hitting like a sharp gust of wind. "What do you mean?"

"You know," she said, her fingers tapping the keys absently. "Mom says you used to make music that made people *feel* stuff. Like, really feel it."

Elias froze. Rachel must've said that in passing, not realizing how those words would land. He forced a smile. "I still play, kiddo. It's just... different now."

Lily tilted her head, studying him with a seriousness that seemed out of place on her small face. "I think you should play the way you want to. Even if it's different."

Her words hung in the air, unsettling in their simplicity.

After Rachel and Lily left, Elias found himself staring at the piano, Lily's comment looping in his head. "Play the way you want to."

He sighed, sitting down on the bench. His fingers hovered over the keys, uncertain, before playing the melody he'd started weeks ago. The notes were tentative, but they felt closer—more him—than they had in a long time.

The following week, Elias met Lily's piano teacher at the community center. She was a petite woman with a quick smile and a tendency to ramble.

"You're Elias, right?" she asked, shaking his hand. "Lily talks about you all the time. Says you're a genius. No pressure, though!"

Elias chuckled awkwardly. "She's sweet. And persistent."

"Oh, absolutely. The other day, she told me I should make my lessons more 'exciting' like yours. I wasn't sure whether to be flattered or offended."

They both laughed, and for the first time in a while, Elias felt at ease.

The teacher handed him a progress report covered in stickers. "She's got a gift, you know. But more than that, she's got heart. That's rare."

Elias nodded, his throat tightening. "Yeah, she's... special."

The teacher hesitated, her smile softening. "She looks up to you. Don't underestimate how much that means."

Her words lingered as Elias walked home, the paper crinkling in his hand. He thought about Lily's unshakable belief in him, her innocent advice to "play the way you want to." It wasn't just sweet—it was grounding, a reminder of the kind of connection he'd almost forgotten was possible.

That evening, Elias sat at his piano, his gaze drifting to the progress report Lily had left behind. Without thinking, he placed it on the music stand, the colorful stickers standing out against the worn wood.

He played again, the melody was fuller this time. It wasn't perfect, but it was his. And as the music filled the room, he felt something shift—a small, stubborn ember of hope reigniting in his chest.

Chapter 8: Echoes in the Silence

Elias stood outside the community center, staring at the chipped green door as if it might bite him. The wind nipped at his neck, but it wasn't the cold that froze him in place. It was the flyer crumpled in his pocket: *"Bipolar Support Group: Share. Listen. Heal."* The words felt as distant as a motivational poster in a dentist's office.

He took a deep breath, rolling his shoulders like he was gearing up for battle. Finally, he stepped inside.

The room was smaller than he'd expected, with a circle of mismatched chairs and a table off to the side holding a coffee pot and a sad little plate of cookies.

Twelve heads turned as he entered, the door squeaking loudly behind him.

"Hi there," said a woman with glasses and a warm, steady voice. "You must be Elias. Come on in. Take a seat anywhere."

He nodded, muttered a quick "Thanks," and slipped into a chair near the edge of the circle, his hands shoved deep in his hoodie pockets.

The first speaker was a man with tattoos creeping up his arms and a shaved head that gleamed under the fluorescent lights. He introduced himself as Nate.

"Last week was rough," Nate said, his voice gravelly but steady. "I got into it with my brother. He says I use my diagnosis as an excuse."

He paused, running a hand over his head. "The thing is, I can see where he's coming from. Sometimes I'm so scared of screwing up that I... just don't do anything at all. And that makes him think I'm lazy, but really, I'm just stuck, you know?"

Elias watched as the woman next to Nate—a red-haired firecracker who called herself Jess—nodded vigorously.

"Stuck is the worst," Jess chimed in. "It's like... you're screaming underwater, but no one hears you. My family's always like, 'You should get out more, do something fun.' And I'm like, 'You think *this* is fun for me?"

The group laughed, and even Elias found himself smirking at the sharp honesty in her tone.

When it was Elias's turn to speak, the group leader—Karen—offered him an encouraging smile.

"You don't have to say much," she said. "Even a sentence can be powerful."

Elias swallowed hard, his heart thudding against his ribcage. "Uh... hi. I'm Elias," he began, his voice barely above a whisper.

"Hi, Elias," the group echoed, their voices warm and welcoming.

He shifted in his seat, his hands fidgeting in his lap. "I guess I'm here because... I don't want to feel so alone with this anymore."

A pause, then Nate nodded. "Man, I get that," he said, his tone serious. "That's why I came here the first time too. It's like... the world doesn't get it, but these people do."

Elias felt the knot in his chest loosen slightly.

As the session continued, Elias listened to more stories, each one carving a small opening in the walls he'd built around himself.

There was Mrs. Patel, an older woman with silver-streaked hair who spoke softly about losing her job after a manic episode. "It's hard to explain to people why you're suddenly calling them at 3 a.m. with business ideas," she said, shaking her head.

And then there was Kevin, a lanky guy in his twenties who fidgeted with his hoodie strings as he spoke. "I dropped out of college twice," he admitted. "The first time was because I was too high to sleep for a week. The second time... I couldn't even get out of bed to go to class."

"Third time's the charm?" Jess asked, her grin was mischievous but kind.

Kevin chuckled. "Here's hoping."

The room buzzed with a strange mix of sadness and humor, and Elias found himself drawn in by the rawness of it all. These weren't rehearsed speeches or sanitized stories. They were messy, awkward, painfully real.

By the end of the session, the circle didn't feel quite as intimidating. He still didn't know anyone well, but their voices lingered in his mind, like threads weaving into a larger tapestry.

As the group dispersed, Karen approached Elias. "I'm glad you came today," she said gently. "It's not easy to take that first step."

"Yeah," he said, his voice quieter than he'd intended. "Thanks for... not making it weird."

Karen laughed, her glasses slipping down her nose. "That's what we're here for."

Walking home, Elias replayed the session in his head. It wasn't perfect—he hadn't shared much, and his nerves still gnawed at him—but something about it felt... right.

He stopped at a park bench, pulling out a folded piece of sheet music from his pocket. It was an unfinished melody he'd been carrying around for weeks, its blank spaces taunting him.

This time, though, he didn't feel stuck.

He pulled out a pen and added a few notes, the lines flowing easily. The melody wasn't polished, but it was real. And for the first time, that felt like enough.

Chapter 9: The Gathering Storm

Elias stared at the small orange pill in his palm, the morning light streaming through his window and catching on its glossy surface. It felt heavier than it should—like it carried every compromise he'd made since his diagnosis. With a sigh, he swallowed it and chased it with water, the familiar bitterness settling on his tongue.

He moved to the piano, his fingers brushing the keys. The notes that emerged were fine, technically perfect, but they felt hollow. The music used to roar through him, unstoppable and alive. Now, it was a faint echo of what it once had been, like listening to a symphony through a wall.

Elias pressed his hands to his temples, frustration bubbling beneath his skin. The medication had steadied him, dulled the highs and muted the lows—but it had also taken something else, something vital.

The knock on the door broke through his spiraling thoughts. Elias opened it to find Noah leaning casually against the frame, his leather jacket slung over one shoulder.

"Elias!" Noah grinned, stepping inside without waiting for an invitation. "How's the maestro today?"

Elias shrugged, closing the door. "Same as always."

Noah dropped onto the couch, his presence filling the room. He had a way of making everything seem smaller and bigger at the same time. "Still popping those little pills?"

Elias bristled. "You mean the meds? Yeah, still on them."

Noah snorted. "Man, those things are creativity killers. Remember last year? That insane jazz piece you wrote? You were *on fire.*"

"Yeah, and I also almost burned my life down in the process," Elias shot back, sharper than he intended.

Noah held up his hands in mock surrender, his grin unrepentant. "Hey, I'm just saying. A little chaos never hurt anyone. Sometimes the price of genius is, well... a little storm."

Elias leaned against the piano, his arms crossed. He wanted to dismiss Noah's words; to tell him he didn't get it. But part of him wondered if he did. There was a thrill to the chaos, a fire that felt unstoppable in the moment. And God, did he miss it.

That night, Elias sat at the piano long after Noah had left. His thoughts churned, cycling between his frustration with the meds and the seductive pull of his old manic energy.

He remembered the nights when the music flowed effortlessly, when inspiration struck like lightning, leaving him breathless and alive. But he also remembered the crash—the hospital, the quiet devastation of realizing how far he'd fallen.

His phone buzzed, breaking the silence. It was Chloe: *Hey, you, okay? Haven't heard from you in a few days.*

Elias stared at the screen, his thumb hovering over the keyboard. He could picture her expression—equal parts concern and annoyance—and it made him smile despite himself.

Yeah, just... thinking, he typed.

Her reply came almost immediately: *Dangerous habit. Wanna talk?*

He hesitated, then typed back: *Maybe later. Thanks, though.*

He put the phone down and looked at the orange pill sitting on the table. It caught the light, small and unassuming, but it felt like it was staring back at him, daring him to make a choice.

The next morning, Elias didn't take the pill.

The day after that, he skipped it again.

At first, the change was subtle. He felt sharper, lighter, as if fog had lifted. The music came easier, the melodies flowing with a fluidity he hadn't felt in months. For the first time in what felt like forever, he sat at the piano and played something that moved him.

But beneath the thrill was a growing unease—a tremor he couldn't quite name.

He brushed it aside, pressing harder on the keys, chasing the feeling of being alive again.

That night, he sat in the dark, his reflection faint in the polished wood of the piano. His chest was tight, his thoughts restless. But when he pressed a chord, the sound vibrated through him, real and full.

For now, the music was enough.

Chapter 10: The Descent

Elias sat motionless in his apartment, staring at the muted glow of the clock on the wall. It ticked quietly, each second a tiny reminder of time slipping past him. The sound, once unnoticeable, now felt like a taunt. The minutes stretched endlessly, the days blending into a colorless fog where morning and night were indistinguishable.

The curtains were drawn tight, shutting out the daylight that felt almost cruel in its brightness. Sunlight didn't belong here, in this cocoon of numbness and neglect. The once-pristine space around him had become a silent reflection of his inner turmoil. Dishes piled up in the sink, forgotten meals hardened into remnants of effort he no longer had the energy to clean.

The piano sat untouched, its sleek surface gathering dust. It loomed in the corner of the room like an accusation, a monument to his paralysis.

Elias tried to stand; his body weighed down by an exhaustion so profound it felt as though his limbs were made of lead. Each movement was a Herculean effort, and even breathing seemed like too much to ask.

The music, his lifeline for as long as he could remember, was now a stranger. It had abandoned him when he needed it most, or maybe he had abandoned it. He couldn't tell anymore.

He sat at the piano, his fingers hovering over the keys, the once-familiar weight of them now alien. He pressed a note—a hollow sound that echoed in the stillness of the room, mocking him with its emptiness.

He used to lose himself in the music, the melodies pouring out effortlessly as though they'd always existed somewhere inside him. Now, the keys felt cold and unyielding, a language he could no longer understand.

Elias rested his hands in his lap, staring at his reflection in the polished wood. *What's wrong with me?* he thought, the question looping endlessly in his mind.

At night, the silence grew louder, pressing in on him like a physical weight. Lying in bed, he stared at the ceiling, the faint hum of the city beyond his window, a cruel reminder that life was still moving, just not his.

His thoughts spiraled, circling around the same questions: *Why can't I just get it together? Why am I like this? What if this is all there is?*

The darkness was suffocating, and even sleep felt like a distant dream. When it came, it was fragmented and restless, filled with vivid nightmares of falling endlessly, the ground never meeting him.

On the rare occasion he ventured outside, the world felt alien. The bright sunlight burned his eyes, and the cacophony of the streets was overwhelming.

At the park, children's laughter cut through the air like glass, a painful reminder of a joy he could no longer touch. He sat on a bench, watching a couple walk by hand, their easy intimacy almost too much to bear.

Even the simplest interactions felt insurmountable. At the grocery store, he avoided the cashier's eyes, afraid they might see the shadows under his own and wonder what had happened to him. He imagined them whispering, *What's wrong with him? Why does he look like that?*

Noah's texts had become less frequent, the once steady stream of jokes and jam session invitations now reduced to the occasional check-in. *Hey, you good? Let's jam sometime.*

Elias stared at the message, his fingers hovering over the screen. He wanted to reply, to say something, anything—but what could he say? *No, I'm not good. I can't even touch the piano without feeling like I'm breaking inside.*

The text went unanswered, like so many before it.

The worst moments came in the dead of night when the stillness became unbearable, and his thoughts took on a darker edge.

The rooftop called him, its dizzying height both terrifying and strangely comforting. He remembered standing there, the wind biting at his face, and the seductive pull of the abyss whispering that it could end the relentless weight he carried.

He thought of Chloe's voice, breaking through the fog, her tear-streaked face etched in his memory. Her hands gripping his arms, steadying him, begging him to step back.

She saved me, he thought, the guilt settling heavy in his chest. *But what if I can't stay saved?*

One evening, after days of silence, Elias found himself sitting at the piano again. His reflection stared back at him from the polished surface, hollow and unfamiliar.

He pressed a single key, the sound echoing through the empty apartment. It was jarring, almost painful, but it broke through the suffocating stillness.

Tears welled up, blurring his vision as he rested his head against the piano. For the first time in weeks, he allowed himself to feel everything—the despair, anger, the fear, the longing for a release he couldn't name.

The tears came slowly at first, then all at once, shaking his body with their force. The room blurred around him, but he didn't move. He let it out, the emotions pouring over him like a wave he couldn't hold back.

When the tears finally subsided, the room looked the same, but something inside him had shifted. The music still felt far away, but he had touched something—a flicker of hope, fragile but real.

He didn't know when, or if, the music would return. But as he sat in the quiet, the faint glow of a candle burned in the dark corners of his mind.

And for now, that was enough.

Chapter 11: The Fall

Elias lay on the couch, staring at the cracks in the ceiling. The soft hum of the refrigerator was the only sound in the room. Outside, the city buzzed with life, but inside, the air felt heavy, suffocating.

He hadn't eaten in over a day, and the coffee cup on the table sat empty, a faint ring staining the surface beneath it. His mind was stuck in a loop, replaying the same thoughts over and over. *You're a failure. You'll never get better. Why even try?*

His eyes drifted to the piano in the corner. It stood untouched, silent. He'd tried to play earlier, desperate to find solace in the music, but his fingers had frozen on the keys. The melodies he used to create so effortlessly now felt distant, unreachable.

The phone buzzed on the coffee table, vibrating against the glass. He ignored it. It buzzed again, insistent.

Finally, with a groan, Elias reached for it. Chloe's name lit up the screen.

He stared at the phone, his thumb hovering over the green icon. Talking felt like an impossible task. The thought of explaining himself, of trying to make her understand, was overwhelming.

The call went to voicemail. A text followed seconds later: *Elias, I'm worried about you. Please call me back.*

He set the phone down, guilt twisting in his chest. Chloe didn't deserve this. But he couldn't bring himself to reach out.

Hours passed, though Elias wasn't sure how many. The oppressive silence of the apartment grew unbearable, pressing in on him from all sides.

Grabbing his coat, he stepped outside. The chilly air hit him like a slap, but it wasn't enough to pull him out of his haze. He walked aimlessly until he found himself at the entrance to his building's rooftop.

The rooftop was quiet, the city lights below glittering like stars against the darkness. The wind whipped around him, sharp and biting, but he barely felt it.

Elias approached the edge, his heart pounding. His hands gripped the cold metal railing, his breath coming in short bursts.

The height was dizzying. For a moment, he imagined what it would feel like to let go. The thought was terrifying, but also strangely comforting.

What if this is the only way to make it all stop?

"Elias!"

Chloe's voice shattered the stillness, sharp and panicked. He turned his head to see her standing at the rooftop entrance, her chest heaving as though she'd sprinted up the stairs.

"What are you doing?" she demanded, her voice trembling.

"Go home, Chloe," he said flatly.

Her eyes widened; fear etched across her face. "No," she said firmly, stepping closer. "I'm not leaving. You don't get to push me away. Not now."

Elias turned back toward the railing, his grip tightening. "I'm tired, Chloe," he said, his voice breaking. "I don't know how to keep doing this."

Her voice softened, though her fear was still palpable. "I know you're tired. But this isn't the way. Please, Elias. Step back. I can't lose you."

Her words pierced through the fog in his mind, cutting through the darkness. He looked at her, saw the tears streaming down her face, the desperation in her eyes.

With a shaky breath, Elias stepped back from the edge.

Chloe was at his side in an instant, wrapping her arms around him tightly. He felt the warmth of her embrace, the steadiness of her heartbeat against his chest.

But she didn't let go for long. Pulling back slightly, she looked at him, her face fierce with determination. "I'm calling an ambulance."

"Chloe, you don't have to—"

"Yes, I do," she interrupted, her voice leaving no room for argument. "This isn't something I can handle on my own. You need help, Elias. Real help."

He didn't protest. The weight of her words settled over him, heavy but undeniable.

She fumbled with her phone, dialing quickly. "Hi, yes. I need an ambulance. My friend... he's suicidal. We're on the rooftop of…" Her voice faltered briefly before she gave their location.

Elias sank to the ground, his back against the wall. Chloe stayed beside him, one hand gripping his tightly as she spoke to the dispatcher.

"It's going to be okay," she whispered after hanging up. "You're going to be okay."

The ambulance's flashing lights painted the rooftop in red and blues. Paramedics moved with practiced efficiency, asking Elias questions he barely registered. Chloe stayed close, her presence grounding him as they guided him down the stairs.

By the time they reached the hospital, the adrenaline had worn off, leaving Elias hollow and numb. But somewhere deep inside, he felt a flicker of something he hadn't in weeks: relief.

He didn't know what came next, but for the first time in a long time, he thought he might be ready to find out.

Chapter 12: Finding the Balance

Elias sat on the hospital bed, staring at the tiled floor. The faint antiseptic smell clung to the air, sharp and sterile, and his fingers fidgeted with the edge of the blanket. The room felt too bright, too white, too open—a stark contrast to the dim, cluttered cocoon of his apartment.

He wasn't sure which was worse: the physical exhaustion pressing down on him or the shame curling in his chest.

The door creaked open, and Dr. Vance stepped in, carrying a clipboard he barely glanced at before pulling a chair closer to Elias. "Good morning," he said, his voice steady but warm. "How are you feeling?"

Elias shrugged; his gaze fixed on his lap. "Like I screwed everything up."

Dr. Vance nodded, letting the silence settle for a moment before speaking. "It takes courage to admit that. But let's talk about why you feel that way."

Elias hesitated, his throat tightening as he searched for the words. "I... stopped taking my meds," he finally said, his voice barely above a whisper.

"Can you tell me why?" Dr. Vance asked gently.

Elias exhaled sharply, the weight of the question pressing on him. "Because I wanted to feel alive again," he admitted. "I thought... I thought the meds were making me dull. Like, yeah, I wasn't crashing anymore, but I wasn't creating either. I wasn't... me."

Dr. Vance leaned forward slightly, his hands resting on his knees. "I understand that fear," he said. "It's something a lot of people struggle with. But let me ask you this: Did stopping the medication bring you closer to the version of yourself you were looking for?"

Elias's chest tightened as the question hit home. "No," he admitted. "It just made everything worse."

Dr. Vance's voice softened. "Elias, the medication isn't about changing who you are. Think of it like tuning an instrument. You've got incredible music inside you, but when it's out of tune, it's hard to hear clearly. The meds help you tune the strings, so you can play the way you want without everything falling apart.

Elias looked up; his eyes met Dr. Vance's for the first time. "But what if I lose... me?"

"You won't," Dr. Vance assured him. "That spark you're afraid of losing. It's still there. We just need to find the balance that works for you."

They talked for over an hour, Elias's apprehension giving way to cautious curiosity. Dr. Vance explained the nuances of different medications, how adjustments could make a difference, and emphasized that Elias wasn't just a patient but a partner in his own care.

"This isn't about forcing you into a mold," Dr. Vance said. "It's about giving you the tools to live the life you want—on your terms."

For the first time in what felt like forever, Elias felt a glimmer of empowerment. “I don’t want to feel like this anymore,” he said quietly. “I want to find that balance.”

“And you will,” Dr. Vance said, his tone firm but kind. “We’ll figure it out together.”

Later, when Chloe arrived, she burst into the room with a mix of relief and exasperation. “You scared the hell out of me, Elias,” she said, her voice cracking as she wrapped her arms around him.

“I’m sorry,” he murmured, his voice muffled against her shoulder.

“You don’t get to be sorry,” she said, pulling back to look him in the eye. “You just have to let me help you. I can’t fix this for you, but I can be here. I can hold on when you can’t.”

Her words hit him like a lifeline tossed into deep water. “I’ll try,” he said, his voice trembling. “I don’t know if I can promise more than that right now, but... I’ll try.”

“That’s enough,” she said, her eyes shining. “That’s all I need.”

That night, after Chloe had left, Elias sat in the quiet of his apartment. The air felt a little less suffocating, though the shadows in the corners still lingered.

He moved to the piano, his fingers brushing the keys. For a moment, he hesitated, the weight of the past few weeks pressing down on him. Then, slowly, he pressed a single note.

The sound was soft, hesitant, but it was real. He pressed another, then another, the beginnings of a melody forming.

The music wasn't perfect. It wasn't the wild, unstoppable force it had once been. But it was his.

As the melody filled the room, Elias felt a flicker of hope—a reminder that even after the storm, there could be music.

Chapter 13: Picking Up the Pieces

Elias sat by the hospital window, staring out at the gray afternoon sky. It had been a week since the rooftop, a week of daily therapy sessions, restless nights, and cautiously measured steps toward stability.

He still remembered the look on Chloe's face when she found him. The fear in her eyes haunted him, a reminder of how close he'd come to breaking up the people he cared about most. He'd replayed that moment a hundred times in his mind, wishing he could erase it, knowing he couldn't.

The faint sound of footsteps pulled him from his thoughts. Dr. Vance appeared in the doorway, clipboard in hand but his expression relaxed. "Good to see you sitting up," he said, settling into the chair beside Elias.

Elias nodded; his hands folded in his lap. "Yeah. It's... better than the bed."

Dr. Vance smiled faintly. "Small steps matter. How are you feeling today?"

Elias hesitated. "I don't know," he admitted. "Some days feel okay. Others feel like I'm stuck in this... fog. I want to get better, but it feels like there's so much to fix."

Dr. Vance leaned forward slightly, his tone calm and steady. "Recovery isn't about fixing everything at once.

It's about taking things one day at a time. Rebuilding is a process, Elias, and you're not doing it alone."

Elias let those words sink in, the weight of them both comforting and daunting.

The next day, Chloe visited. She arrived with her usual energy, though it was tinged with something softer, more cautious.

"Hey," she said, peeking around the door with a tentative smile.

"Hey," Elias replied, his voice quieter than usual.

She carried a small bag, setting it down on the table beside him. "I brought you something. Well, two things."

He raised an eyebrow as she pulled out a familiar leather-bound notebook and a bag of chocolate-covered pretzels.

"I thought you might want this back," she said, handing him the notebook. "You left it at my place."

Elias took it, running his fingers over the worn cover. The pages inside were filled with fragments of melodies, lyrics, and hastily scribbled thoughts—some coherent, others not.

"And the pretzels?" he asked, a faint smile tugging at his lips.

"Because hospital food is terrible," she said, grinning.

Elias chuckled softly; the sound surprised even him. "Thanks, Chloe. For... everything."

Her smile faded slightly, replaced by something more serious. "You don't have to thank me. I just... I'm glad you're here."

That night, Elias sat by the window, the notebook opens on his lap. He flipped through the pages, pausing on a half-written melody he'd started months ago. The notes were messy, scattered, but they felt like a starting point.

He picked up the pencil Chloe had brought him, hesitating for a moment before sketching a new line of notes. The melody was soft and hesitant, but it carried a thread of hope.

For the first time in a long time, he didn't feel like the music was mocking him. It felt like it was waiting—patient, forgiving.

The days passed slowly, each one marked by small victories: stepping outside for fresh air, laughing at one of Chloe's sarcastic comments, sharing his thoughts with Dr. Vance without holding back.

It wasn't easy. There were moments when the weight of it all felt like too much, when he wanted to retreat into the silence of his mind. But each time, he reminded himself of the people who had stood by him—Chloe, Dr. Vance, even the paramedics who'd saved him.

On his last day at the hospital, Chloe arrived early, her arms filled with flowers.

"Don't worry, I didn't go overboard," she said, setting the bouquet down on the table. "Just enough to make your apartment look less... depressing."

Elias smirked. "You're assuming I'll even leave them alive long enough to do that."

"Optimism is part of my charm," she quipped, but her smile softened as she added, "I'm proud of you, Elias."

The words caught him off guard, leaving him momentarily speechless.

"Thanks," he said finally. "For... everything. I mean it."

Chloe shrugged, brushing off the sentiment with a casual wave of her hand. "That's what friends are for."

As Elias stepped into his apartment later that evening, the silence felt different—less oppressive, more welcoming. He placed the bouquet on the counter and set his notebook on the piano, its presence a quiet reminder of where he'd been and where he wanted to go.

Sitting down, he opened the notebook to the melody he'd started in the hospital. His fingers brushed the keys, hesitant but ready.

The first notes rang out, soft and deliberate, filling the room with a fragile but unmistakable sense of hope.

Chapter 14: A Fragile Harmony

The concert hall hummed with quiet anticipation. The rows of seats were nearly full, the audience leaning forward in their chairs, whispering softly. The air crackled with electric energy that mirrored Elias's own mix of excitement and trepidation.

He sat beside Chloe, her hand resting lightly on his. Her touch was steady, a silent reassurance that sent warmth radiating through him.

"This feels surreal," Elias whispered, his eyes scanning the grand stage ahead.

Chloe smiled gently. "It's your first outing since... everything. Take it in. You've earned this."

Her words were simple, but they carried a weight that anchored Elias.

The lights dimmed, and a hush fell over the room. The spotlight illuminated a lone pianist on stage, his fingers poised above the keys.

The first notes filled the hall, a delicate cascade that swelled into a powerful wave of sound. Elias closed his eyes, letting the music wash over him. Each note seemed to tug at something buried deep within—a longing, a sorrow, a fragile hope.

He felt the familiar ache of the past—the struggles, the loss, the moments when he thought the music within him had been silenced forever. But woven into the melody was something else: resilience, a stubborn will to keep going despite it all.

Elias glanced at Chloe; her face bathed in the soft glow of the stage lights. Her eyes shimmered, reflecting a mix of emotions—sadness, joy, pride. He saw his own journey reflected in her gaze, a shared understanding that didn't need words.

As the pianist's hands danced across the keys, Elias imagined himself sitting there, creating a melody that could speak what he struggled to say out loud. The music seemed to whisper to him: *You're still here. You're still whole, even in your brokenness.*

After the concert, they walked hand-in-hand through the moonlit streets. The air was crisp, carrying the faint scent of autumn leaves.

Chloe broke the silence first. "That music... it felt like a conversation. Like it was telling a story."

Elias nodded. "A story of darkness and light. Of searching for something steady to hold onto."

She squeezed his hand. "It's what you do with your music too, Elias. It's what you've always done."

He glanced at her, surprised. "Even when I felt like I'd lost it?"

"Especially then," she said firmly. "Your music has always been about the truth. And even when it's raw, messy, or painful, it's still beautiful. Because it's you."

Her words settled over him, a quiet affirmation he hadn't known he needed.

Back at his apartment, the silence felt different—not empty but brimming with possibility. Elias moved instinctively to the piano, his fingers grazing the worn keys.

Chloe perched on the edge of the couch, watching him with quiet anticipation.

He closed his eyes, letting the emotions of the evening settle. The notes came slowly at first, soft and hesitant. But as the melody grew, it became something more—something that carried both the weight of his struggles and the lightness of his hope.

Each note was a piece of his journey: the manic highs, the crushing lows, the fear, the love, the resilience. He poured himself into the music, creating a tapestry of sound that was raw and honest, a reflection of the person he was becoming.

When he finished, the silence that followed was profound. Chloe wiped a tear from her cheek, her voice soft but steady. "That... was incredible."

Elias let out a breath he didn't realize he'd been holding. "It felt... real. Like I finally said what I've been trying to say all this time."

"You did," Chloe said, crossing the room to sit beside him. "And I think the world needs to hear it."

That night, as Elias lay in bed, the melody still lingered in his mind, echoing like a quiet promise. He didn't know what the future would hold—there would be challenges, no doubt. But for the first time in a long time, he felt ready to face them.

Because even amidst the chaos, he had found his fragile harmony.

Chapter 15: The Weight of Care

Chloe sat at the kitchen table, her fingers wrapped around a mug of tea had gone cold. The rhythmic ticking of the wall clock filled the silence, each second a small reminder of how much time she spent worrying about Elias.

She glanced at her phone, half-expecting a message, but the screen remained dark. The absence of his texts used to frustrate her—now, it terrified her.

A soft knock on the door broke her thoughts. She opened it to find Sarah, her best friend since college, holding a bottle of wine in one hand and a sympathetic smile.

"I figured you could use this," Sarah said, stepping inside and placing the bottle on the counter.

Chloe let out a tired laugh. "You're a mind reader."

"Nope," Sarah replied, pouring the wine into two mismatched glasses. "I just know you well enough to know when you're drowning."

They sat on the couch, the glasses of wine balanced on the coffee table. Chloe took a deep sip, the warmth spreading through her chest.

"How's he doing?" Sarah asked gently.

Chloe sighed, her shoulders slumping. "Better, I think. He's out of the hospital, at least. But it's like... I don't know. He's here, but sometimes it feels like he's still so far away."

Sarah nodded; her expression thoughtful. "That's hard. For both of you."

"It is," Chloe admitted. "And I love him—I do. But sometimes, I feel so... drained. Like I'm carrying both of us, and I don't know if I'm strong enough to keep doing it."

Sarah reached out, placing a hand over Chloe's. "It's okay to feel that way, you know. Loving someone doesn't mean you have to be invincible."

Chloe's eyes stung with tears. "I just want him to be okay, Sarah. I want him to feel alive again. But what if... what if I'm not enough?"

"You don't have to be everything," Sarah said softly. "You're part of his support system, but you're not the whole thing. It's okay to set boundaries. To take care of yourself too."

Chloe nodded, but the words settled heavily in her chest.

Later that night, after Sarah had left, Chloe stood in the doorway of the living room, watching Elias at the piano.

His back was to her, his shoulders hunched as his fingers moved hesitantly over the keys. The melody was soft, almost fragile, but it was there. It was real.

She walked in quietly, sitting on the edge of the couch. "That's beautiful," she said softly.

Elias turned, startled. "I didn't hear you come in."

"I didn't want to interrupt," she said, smiling faintly.

He hesitated, his gaze dropping to the keys. "It's not much. Just something I've been working on."

"It's enough," Chloe said, her voice firm. "It's you."

He looked at her then, his expression a mix of gratitude and uncertainty. "I don't know how to thank you," he said. "For... everything."

"You don't have to thank me," she replied. "But you do have to let me in. You don't have to do this alone, Elias. I'm here, but you have to let me be here."

He nodded, his eyes glistening. "I'll try."

That night, Chloe sat in her room, flipping through an old journal she'd started years ago. The pages were filled with scribbled notes about her dreams, her fears, her hopes for the future.

She paused on a page she'd written after meeting Elias for the first time. *He has this energy about him,* she'd written. *Like he sees the world in colors no one else can. I don't know where this is going, but I think I want to find out.*

The memory brought a small, bittersweet smile to her lips. Elias had always been complicated, but he'd also brought so much light into her life.

Closing the journal, Chloe placed it on her nightstand and turned off the light. The weight of care was heavy, but it was one she wasn't ready to let go of. Not yet.

Chapter 16: Shadows of Doubt

Elias sat on a bench in the park, the crisp autumn air carrying the scent of fallen leaves and distant coffee stands. Around him, the world moved on—children raced each other down the path, a dog barked playfully at a flock of pigeons, and a street musician strummed a guitar softly under a tree.

But Elias felt disconnected, as though the vibrant world around him was happening in a different dimension.

His fingers traced the edges of the notebook in his lap, the leather cover worn smoothly from years of use. Inside were the beginnings of a new composition, the first real attempt he'd made in months. The notes were tentative, unsure, much like himself.

The melody haunted him—a reflection of the uncertainty he carried. Could he trust himself again? Could he trust the music?

He looked up at the sky, the clouds drifting slowly across the pale blue expanse. *One day at a time,* he reminded himself. It was something Dr. Vance had said, but the words felt impossibly large in that moment.

The sound of a text notification broke through Elias's thoughts. It was from Chloe: *What's on your mind today?*

Elias stared at the screen for a moment, debating how much to share. Finally, he typed: *Just trying to figure out where I go from here.*

Her response came almost immediately: *Wherever it is, you don't have to figure it out alone.*

A small smile tugged at his lips. Chloe always had a way of saying exactly what he needed to hear without making it feel like pressure.

Thanks, he replied. *That means a lot.*

Later that afternoon, Elias sat at the piano in his small studio, his fingers gliding over the keys as he prepared for his student's arrival. Teaching had always been a strange mix of joy and trepidation—he loved sharing his passion for music, but he worried about the expectations his students might have.

When Lily arrived, she bumped into the room with her usual enthusiasm. "Hi, Uncle Elias!"

"Hey, kiddo," he said, ruffling her hair. "You ready to learn something new?"

"Always," she said, her eyes sparkling.

As they worked through a simple piece, Elias noticed her gaze lingering on him. Finally, she asked, "Uncle Elias, are you happy?"

The question caught him off guard. He faltered, his fingers slipping off the keys. "What makes you ask that?"

Lily shrugged; her expression thoughtful. "You seem... different lately. Not bad, simply different."

Elias took a deep breath, considering his words. “I’m working on it,” he said finally. “Being happy, I mean. It’s not always easy, but I’m trying.”

Lily nodded as if she understood more than her seven years should allow. “That’s good. Mom says trying is what matters.”

Elias smiled, the simplicity of her wisdom grounding him. “Your mom’s a smart lady.”

After Lily left, the studio was quiet again. Elias sat at the piano, replaying the conversation in his mind. The vulnerability of her question lingered, pushing him to confront his own uncertainty.

He opened his notebook, staring at the unfinished melody. Picking up a pencil, he began sketching new notes, his hand moving almost instinctively.

The music grew slowly, weaving a story of hesitation and hope. It wasn’t perfect, but it was real.

That evening, as Elias walked home, the streetlights flickered on, casting long shadows across the pavement. He paused by a café where a violinist played on the sidewalk, her bow gliding gracefully across the strings.

The melody was simple but poignant, cutting through the noise of the city. Elias stood there for a moment, letting the music wash over him.

It reminded him of something Dr. Vance had said during their last session: *“Progress doesn’t have to be loud or fast. Sometimes, it's quiet and steady, like a heartbeat."*

Elias placed a few coins in the violinist's open case and continued on his way. The shadows of doubt still clung to him, but they felt less suffocating now, less all-consuming.

He didn't know what tomorrow would bring, but he was starting to believe that he could face it—one note, one step at a time.

Chapter 17: Navigating the Gray Areas

The chair in Dr. Vance's office was comfortable enough, but Elias still couldn't help shifting restlessly. The quiet hum of the air conditioner filled the space as sunlight streamed through the window, highlighting a framed photo on the desk—a serene lakeside scene.

Elias's gaze lingered on the photo as he spoke. "It's like... I'm constantly walking on eggshells. Every time I feel good, I start wondering when it's all going to fall apart again."

Dr. Vance nodded; his expression thoughtful. "That's a common feeling after what you've been through. Recovery isn't linear, Elias. It's messy. There will be ups and downs, but it's about learning to manage those moments instead of fearing them."

Elias leaned back; his arms crossed. "I know that, logically. But knowing doesn't make it easier. It's like every good day comes with a price tag—a reminder that the bad days aren't far behind."

Dr. Vance tilted his head slightly. "Have you ever tried shifting that perspective? Instead of seeing the good days as a temporary reprieve, what if you looked at them as evidence that better moments are possible, even if they're not constant?"

Elias frowned, the words settling uncomfortably. "I don't know. It feels... fake. Like I'm just trying to trick myself into being optimistic."

"That's not unusual," Dr. Vance said gently. "Optimism doesn't have to be about ignoring the challenges. It's about acknowledging them while also making space for hope. Think of it like music—it's not about avoiding dissonance entirely, but about how you resolve it."

The analogy gave Elias a pause. "So, it's like composing? You have to figure out how the bad notes fit into the whole piece?"

"Exactly," Dr. Vance said, smiling. "Sometimes those dissonant moments add depth to the melody. They're not mistakes—they're part of the story."

The session continued, and Elias found himself opening up more than he expected. He talked about the fear that gripped him every time he sat at the piano, the worry that the music wouldn't come back.

"It's like... it used to flow so easily. Now, even when I play something halfway decent, I can't help but wonder if it's the last time."

Dr. Vance leaned forward slightly; his tone measured. "What would happen if you stopped putting so much pressure on the music? What if it didn't have to carry the weight of everything you're feeling?"

Elias blinked, the question catching him off guard. "I don't know. I've always used music to process things. It's how I've made sense of the world."

"Maybe it still can be," Dr. Vance said. "But it doesn't have to be perfect, and it doesn't have to happen all at once. Sometimes, just sitting with the process—without expectations—can be enough."

Elias nodded slowly, the idea settling into a quiet corner of his mind.

As the session wound down, Elias glanced at the clock, surprised by how quickly the time had passed.

"So, what's the plan?" he asked, his voice laced with cautious curiosity.

Dr. Vance smiled. "The plan is to keep experimenting. Try to view setbacks as data, not failures. Keep leaning into the things that ground you—music, therapy, Chloe—and give yourself permission to move at your own pace."

Elias stood, slipping his hands into his pockets. "I'll try," he said, the words hesitant but sincere.

"That's all anyone can ask," Dr. Vance replied.

Walking home, Elias felt the autumn breeze tugging at his jacket. He passed a park where a group of kids played tag, their laughter echoing through the crisp air.

For a moment, he stopped, watching the scene unfold. The simplicity of their joy felt foreign but magnetic, tugging at something deep inside him.

When he reached his apartment, he didn't head straight to the piano like he might have in the past. Instead, he picked up his notebook and wrote a single line: *It doesn't have to be perfect—it just has to be real.*

It wasn't a melody yet, but it was a start.

Chapter 18: Facing the Music

Elias stood in the doorway of the music classroom, his fingers gripping the edge of the doorframe. The room smelled faintly of wood polish and sheet music, a familiar scent that should have calmed him. Instead, it set his heart racing.

The piano sat in the center of the room, gleaming under the overhead lights. He had spent countless hours teaching here, watching students wrestle with melodies until they found their rhythm. But now, the room felt different—he felt different.

He stepped inside slowly, the echo of his footsteps bouncing off the walls.

"Elias?"

He turned to see Ms. Harper, the school's administrative assistant, peeking around the corner. Her expression was kind but hesitant, as though she wasn't sure how to approach him.

"Hi, Ms. Harper," Elias said, his voice strained but polite.

"Welcome back," she said softly. "It's good to see you here again."

Elias nodded, unsure how to respond. He wondered how much she knew—how much anyone here knew. The thought made his stomach twist.

As the day unfolded, the nerves didn't subside entirely, but they became manageable. By the time his first student arrived, Elias had found a rhythm—greeting each child, easing them into their lessons with patience and encouragement.

One student, a shy boy named Marcus, struggled with a simple scale, his small fingers fumbling over the keys.

"Take your time," Elias said gently. "It's not about getting it perfect the first time. It's about learning how to try."

Marcus glanced up at him, his eyes wide. "Is that what you do?"

Elias paused, the question hitting deeper than he expected. "Yeah," he said after a moment. "Every day."

During a break, Elias sat at his desk, flipping through sheet music. The buzz of the hallway outside was a distant hum, but it only reminded him of the world he was slowly stepping back into.

He picked up his phone, hesitating before texting Chloe: *First day back. It's harder than I thought.*

Her reply came quickly: *Hard doesn't mean bad. I'm proud of you.*

He smiled faintly, the words settling over him like a quiet reassurance.

At the end of the day, Elias lingered in the classroom, his fingers brushing the piano keys. He played a few notes, the sound echoing softly in the empty room.

The melody grew, tentative at first, but it began to take shape—a simple, hopeful tune.

He didn't notice Ms. Harper standing in the doorway until she spoke. "That's beautiful."

Elias turned, startled. "Oh, I didn't see you there."

She smiled. "You've still got it, you know. The music, the connection—it's still there. And so are we. Don't forget that."

Her words caught him off guard, but they lingered long after she left.

Walking home, Elias thought about her comment. He had spent so much time fearing judgment, convinced that his struggles had marked him as broken in the eyes of others. But maybe that wasn't entirely true.

He paused outside a café where a young woman played the violin, her bow moving gracefully over the strings. The music was raw, imperfect, but filled with emotion. A small crowd had gathered, their faces alight with appreciation.

Elias placed a few coins in her case, the clink of metal barely audible over the music. For the first time in weeks, he felt a spark of something he hadn't dared name: hope.

That night, Elias sat at his piano, opening his notebook to the unfinished melody he'd started days ago. He played it slowly, letting the notes flow, not worrying about perfection.

The music filled the room, carrying with it the weight of his doubts and the fragile beginnings of his resilience.

As he closed the piano lid, he glanced at the notebook. At the bottom of the page, he wrote: *It's not about being flawless. It's about being real.*

Chapter 19: Finding My Voice

Elias sat backstage, his fingers tapping nervously on his knee. The auditorium buzzed with quiet energy, the murmur of the crowd just audibles through the heavy curtain.

He glanced at the program in his hand, his name printed near the bottom: *Elias March—A Personal Journey Through Music and Mental Health.*

The words stared back at him, bold and unflinching. He had agreed to this weeks ago when Chloe convinced him it was time to share his story. But now, under the harsh backstage lights, the weight of what he was about to do felt unbearable.

“What if no one understands?” he muttered to himself.

Chloe appeared at his side, as if summoned by his thoughts. She crouched down, her green eyes locking onto his.

“Hey,” she said softly, placing a hand on his shoulder. “You’ve got this.”

Elias let out a shaky laugh. “I’m not so sure. What if I mess it up? What if they think I’m just... broken?”

Her grip on his shoulder tightened. "You're not broken, Elias. You're human. And your story matters. Trust me—there's someone out there who needs to hear it."

He nodded, swallowing the lump in his throat. Chloe had a way of making things seem possible, even when he doubted himself.

The lights dimmed, and the host's voice echoed through the hall. "Our next speaker is someone who uses music not just as a passion, but as a way to navigate life's challenges. Please welcome Elias March."

Applause rippled through the room as Elias stepped onto the stage, his heart pounding. The piano sat in the spotlight, its black surface gleaming under the lights.

He sat down slowly, his hands hovering over the keys.

"Hi," he began, his voice trembling. He cleared his throat and tried again. "Hi. My name is Elias, and for a long time, I thought I had to be perfect to matter. I thought the only way I could be seen was through my music.

"But life doesn't work that way. And sometimes, the things we love—our passions, our dreams—can feel out of reach when we're struggling."

He paused, his gaze drifting across the audience. Faces stared back at him—some curious, some expectant, some already nodding in quiet understanding.

Elias pressed the first chord: a low, resonant F major, followed by a gentle A minor progression. The notes floated through the room, soft and tentative, like the opening lines of a story yet to unfold.

"A few months ago, I was in a very dark place," he said, his voice blending with the melody. "I didn't think I'd ever make it back to this stage, or to any stage. But I'm here, and I want to tell you something I've learned: You don't have to have all the answers to keep going. You just have to take one step. And then another."

The melody shifted, climbing into an arpeggiated sequence that mimicked the cautious climb of his words. The right hand played a hopeful, rising phrase in C major, while the left grounded it with a steady bassline.

"For me, music has always been my way of making sense of the world," Elias continued, his hands finding a melancholic yet steady refrain. "But it's not just about the music. It's about the people who've stood by me—my friends, my family, my therapist. They reminded me that it's okay to ask for help. That it's okay to lean on others when the weight feels too heavy."

The notes softened, resolving into a simple, heartfelt E major chord that lingered in the stillness of the hall.

Elias played the final notes, letting them linger before turning back to the microphone.

"If you're struggling, I want you to know you're not alone. There's no shame in fighting for yourself, in asking for what you need. And if there's one thing I've learned, it's that even in the darkest moments, there's still music waiting to be found."

The applause started softly, then grew louder, swelling like the crescendo of a symphony. Elias stood, his chest tight with a mix of relief and pride.

As he stepped off the stage, Chloe was waiting in the wings. She wrapped him in a hug, her voice muffled against his shoulder. "You were amazing."

He pulled back, his smile shaky but real. "I don't know if it was amazing, but it was honest."

"And that's what people needed," she said firmly.

That night, as Elias sat at his piano, he replayed the melody he had performed, his fingers moving instinctively. It wasn't perfect, but it was real—a reflection of everything he'd been through and the hope that still lingered on the horizon.

For the first time, Elias felt like he wasn't just playing music. He was sharing it. And in that sharing, he found something he hadn't dared to hope for: connection.

Chapter 20: A Symphony of Selves

Elias sat at his piano, the morning sunlight streaming through the window and pooling on the worn keys. His notebook lay open on the stand, filled with half-finished melodies and scribbled lyrics.

He played a tentative chord, letting the sound linger before adding a descending phrase in minor tones. It felt raw and unpolished, but it spoke to something deep within him—a quiet acceptance of the scars he carried.

For years, music had been his escape, a way to run from the chaos in his mind. Now, it felt different. It wasn't an escape anymore—it was a dialogue, a conversation between the fractured parts of himself.

That afternoon, Elias met Chloe at a café near the park. She greeted him with her usual energy, sliding a steaming cup of coffee across the table.

"You look like you've been up all-night composing," she said, her tone teasing but affectionate.

"Not all night," Elias replied, a faint smile tugging at his lips. "Just... most of it."

Chloe raised an eyebrow. "Good thing I brought reinforcements," she said, pulling a chocolate croissant from her bag and placing it on his plate.

Elias chuckled softly, shaking his head. "You know me too well."

"Someone has to," she said, her expression softening. "How's the piece coming along?"

"It's... complicated," Elias admitted. "But I think that's the point. It's not supposed to be perfect—it's supposed to be honest."

Chloe nodded, her eyes shining. "Honest suits you."

Later, Elias sat in a small, packed auditorium, his notebook in hand. He was attending a mental health panel as both a listener and a participant. The speakers on stage shared their stories of resilience, and Elias found himself nodding along, their words resonating deeply.

When it was his turn to speak, he stood, his palms slightly damp.

"Hi, I'm Elias," he began, his voice steady despite the nerves bubbling beneath the surface. "I'm a composer, a teacher, and I have bipolar disorder."

The room was quiet, but it wasn't an uncomfortable silence. It felt... open.

"For a long time, I thought those two things—being an artist and having this diagnosis—were at odds with each other. But now, I see them as part of the same melody. The highs and lows, the chaos, and the calm—they're all part of me. And that's okay."

He paused, glancing down at the notebook in his hands. "I've learned that recovery isn't about erasing the hard parts. It's about finding harmony within them. And it's about letting others in, even when it feels impossible."

Applause rippled through the room as Elias sat back down. A young man approached him afterward, his hands tucked nervously in his pockets.

"Hey," the man said, his voice quiet. "I just wanted to say... your story really meant a lot to me. I've been struggling with something similar, and hearing you talk about it... it helps."

Elias felt a lump rise in his throat, but he managed a smile. "Thank you. That means more than you know."

Back home, Elias returned to the piano. The notebook on the stand now felt like a reflection of his journey—messy, imperfect, but undeniably real.

He played the melody he'd been working on, weaving in the dissonance that had once frightened him. The notes clashed briefly before resolving into something rich and layered, a testament to the complexity of his life.

As the final chord rang out, Elias leaned back, letting the sound settle. The music wasn't just an escape anymore—it was a bridge, connecting him to the world and to himself.

He glanced at a sticky note Chloe had left on the corner of the piano. It read: *"The world needs your music. Don't keep it waiting."*

Elias smiled, the words echoing in his mind.

He wasn't running anymore. He was here, present, creating not just music but meaning.

And for the first time in years, Elias felt like he was exactly where he was meant to be.

Chapter 21: Coda

The sunlight streamed through the window, illuminating the piano's polished surface and the scattered pages of sheet music on the stand. Elias sat in the familiar seat, his fingers resting lightly on the keys.

The room was quiet, saved for the occasional rustle of paper as the breeze played through the open window. But the stillness no longer felt oppressive. It felt... open.

Elias pressed a single note, letting the sound linger. *There was a time when silence terrified me,* he thought. *Now, it feels like a canvas—empty, but full of possibility.*

His journey had been anything but linear. The highs and lows had left marks on him, but those marks no longer felt like wounds. They were part of his story; written into the music he created.

He opened his notebook, flipping through pages of melodies that spanned months of struggle and resilience. Each fragment carried the weight of a moment—a chord progression born from despair, a rhythm echoing hope, a harmony that whispered forgiveness.

Elias smiled faintly, stopping on a half-finished melody he'd started the night after his first advocacy talk. His hands moved instinctively over the keys, bringing the notes to life.

The piece began softly, the opening chords tentative and searching. A minor progression gave way to a cascade of arpeggios, each one rising like a question: *Who am I? Where am I going?*

Chloe appeared in the doorway; her silhouette framed by the late afternoon sun. She watched quietly for a moment before stepping into the room.

"That's new," she said, her voice warm.

Elias glanced up, his fingers still moving. "It's something I've been working on," he said. "Not sure if it's finished yet."

Chloe smiled, perching on the edge of the piano bench beside him. "Does it need to be?"

Her question hung in the air, and Elias let out a soft laugh. "No, I guess not."

As he played, Chloe rested a hand on his arm. "Remember when you stopped mid-lesson because the notes didn't feel right?" she said, her tone light but nostalgic. "You told me you'd forgotten how to find the music."

He nodded, his gaze drifting to the sheet music in front of him. "It feels like that was a lifetime ago."

"That's because it was," she said, her voice steady. "You've rewritten the whole thing, Elias. And it's beautiful."

That evening, Elias walked through the park, the melody from the piano still lingering in his mind. The laughter of children and the rustling of leaves filled the air, blending into a symphony of everyday life.

He stopped by a fountain, watching the sunlight play across the water. In the distance, a street performer strummed a guitar, the chords rich and imperfect but alive with emotion.

Elias smiled. He wasn't chasing perfection anymore. He wasn't running from the past or fearing the future. He was here, in the present, embracing the harmony of everything he was and everything he could be.

When he returned home, the room was bathed in the soft glow of the evening sun. He sat at the piano, opening his notebook to the blank page he'd left waiting.

With a deep breath, Elias placed his hands on the keys and began to play. The music wasn't finished—it probably never would be. But that was okay.

Because life, like music, wasn't about perfection. It was about the moments, the connections, the pauses, and the crescendos that made it uniquely his.

The Dance I Dance

(Verse 1)

Sunrise in my mind, a spark that feels so rare
Colors crash together, like fireworks in the air
Ideas rush and tumble, too wild for me to bear
But just beyond the brilliance, shadows linger there

(Chorus)

This is the dance I dance, the rhythm I can't ignore
The soaring highs, the crashing lows, the push and pull of more
A fragile step, a careful sway, a battle at my core
The beauty in the chaos, a truth I can't restore

(Verse 2)

The darkness settles in, like a storm that knows my name
It whispers doubts and fears, its voice a steady flame
The world becomes so distant, the silence feeds my shame
But through the cracks, a light breaks in—a flicker I reclaim

(Chorus)

This is the dance I dance, the rhythm I can't ignore
The soaring highs, the crashing lows, the push and pull of more
A fragile step, a careful sway, a battle at my core
The beauty in the chaos, a truth I can't restore

(Bridge)

I've stumbled through the darkness, but I've found my way to stand

The music in my chest reminds me who I am
Each note a step to healing, each chord a guiding hand
The dance is mine to master, the symphony unplanned

(Chorus)

This is the dance I dance, the rhythm I can't ignore
The soaring highs, the crashing lows, the push and pull of more
A fragile step, a careful sway, a battle at my core
The beauty in the chaos, a truth I can't restore

(Outro)

This is my melody, imperfect but it's real
A harmony of scars and hope, the way I choose to heal
With every note I write, I face the fight, I feel
This is the dance I dance—the rhythm that I steal

Acknowledgement

All praise to Allah, the Most Merciful, for His infinite blessings and guidance throughout this journey.

To my parents: Shamshad and Abdul Majid, thank you for your endless love, support, and prayers.

To my readers: This book is a testament to your courage and resilience. Thank you for trusting me with your time and for joining me on this journey.

About the Author

Dr. Shabinabegam (Shabina) Sheth has always believed that mental health care is about more than just treatment—it's about listening, connecting, and sometimes holding space for the occasional nervous giggle during therapy. As a psychiatrist who specializes in working with children, adolescents, and families, she's spent years guiding her patients through the highs, the lows, and the awkward middle bits in between.

Her journey began at Government Medical College, Surat, where she discovered two important things: her calling to psychiatry and that instant coffee can taste like optimism at 2 a.m. During her time at NIMHANS, she led digital health initiatives to bring mental health care to rural communities, learning that sometimes the smallest interventions make the biggest difference. Her work earned her the Best Poster Award—and while meeting the Vice President of India was a thrill, her proudest achievement was finding the confidence to pronounce "tele-ECHO" correctly during interviews.

Her adventures eventually led her to London, where she's now a Child and Adolescent Psychiatrist at the Tavistock and Portman NHS Foundation Trust. She's become quite skilled at juggling complex cases—and occasionally juggling Lego pieces, thanks to her two-year-old son, Muhammed Khizar Ibrahim, who believes pillow forts are serious business.

When she's not advocating for compassionate mental health care or navigating toddler negotiations, Dr. Sheth enjoys creating spaces where everyone—big or small—feels safe, understood, and heard. And when all else fails, she believes there's nothing quite like a good cup of chai and a long, deep breath.

A story of music, mental health, and the unbreakable strength of the human spirit.

www.ingramcontent.com/pod-product-compliance
Ingram Content Group UK Ltd.
Pitfield, Milton Keynes, MK11 3LW, UK
UKHW021409190726
13845UKWH00028B/982

9 789334 226478